Finney's Story

For Adam, Halle and Skyla.
"Daring to dream, always." – A.W.

For Adam, Mildred and Maxwell – C.C.

Huge thanks go to 'The Fox's Den' judges –
Jacob Hayhurst, Angus Holmes, Bobby Holmes and Grace Gorman.

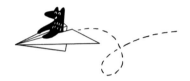

Finney's Story is a uclanpublishing book

First published in Great Britain in 2020 by
uclanpublishing
University of Central Lancashire
Preston, PR1 2HE, UK

978-1-9129794-8-6

1 3 5 7 9 10 8 6 4 2

Printed and bound in Great Britain by Page Bros Ltd, Mile Cross Ln, Norwich NR6 6SA

Finney's Story

Alana Washington & Charlotte Caswell
Read by Sarah-Ann Kennedy

uclanpublishing

" Hang on a minute
Surely **anyone** can read
your book, not just **foxes**? '

" Ah, **good point.**

Everyone will
want to read this

MASTERPIECE "

"Ok – let me have another crack at this...

...

...

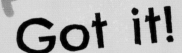

Got it! This is my book for **everyone!**"

"Nailed it! High five!"

" Sooo... what's this book **about** then?

Well?**"**

" I just got so excited about having my own book that, well, I didn't quite get to the **writing** part yet.

But don't worry, I've got **hundreds** of ideas.**"**

"**FANTASTIC,** Finney

Let's hear one then."

"Shall we have lunch first?"

"Ok ok, you're all business today.

Here we go then,
there's this fox who has

**horrible
stepsisters**

that try and stop her going to a **ball** to see this **fox prince** who... **"**

" Hold on a minute isn't that **Cinderella?**

Finney, don't you have any **ORIGINAL** ideas? **"**

"Right.

There's these three brothers, they're **PIGS** actually, and completely mad about **house building..."**

"Come on, Finney! Are you **KIDDING** me? None of these ideas are yours!"

"Calm down. It's not as easy as it sounds. Maybe there just **aren't any original** stories left?

I was just so sure I had a story **bursting** to get out"

"That's **great.**

But just to be on the
safe side,
perhaps we should
visit the **library.**

You know,
just to check your
original ideas
don't happen to be,
um, already in there."

"So I guess you were right. All the original stories are gone."

"I know! There were **HUNDREDS** of books. Rows and rows.

How can there possibly be any story ideas left?

Why did we go there? Why? WHY?"

"I did notice something **weird** though.

I wasn't in **any** of those books."

"Yeah, you're right... In fact, I'm starting to wonder **if we've got this all wrong.**"

"I'm listening."

"Maybe the original story I've been looking for isn't in the library because... **I haven't written it yet!**"

"You've lost me?"

“*MY* STORY!”

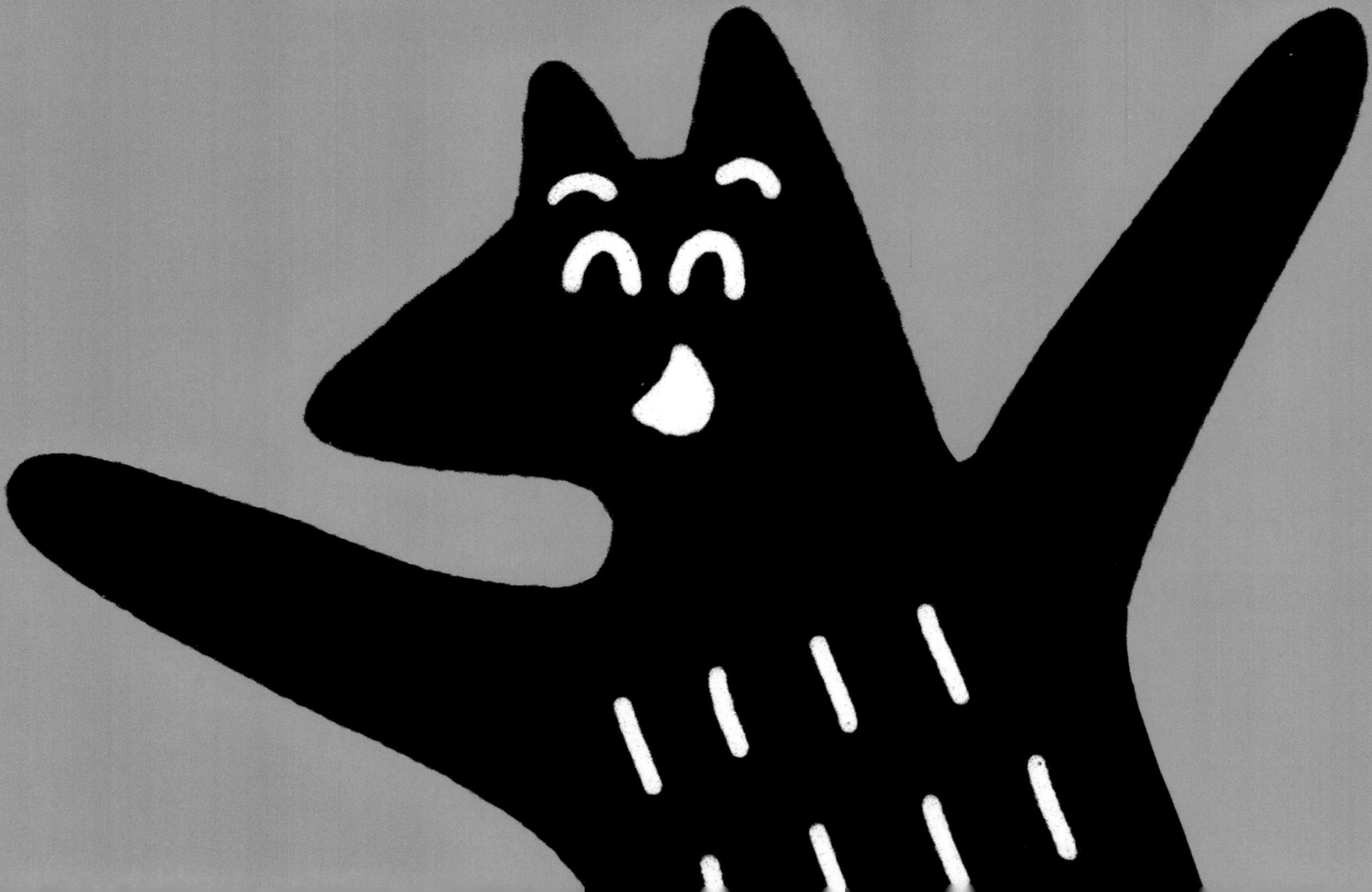

"Ohhh, ha ha.
Of course – yes!
Your story.

So, what you're saying is, we all
have a story to tell – OUR OWN!
Genius! And completely original."

"Why thank you very much."

"I knew I was an **IDEAS MACHINE.**

Right, I better get writing.
How's this?

"There once was a very **good-looking** fox who was **extremely popular.** A **genius,** some would say. Everybody **loved** the way..."

uclanpublishing

HAVE YOU EVER WONDERED HOW BOOKS ARE MADE?

UCLan Publishing are based in the North of England and involve BA Publishing and MA Publishing students from the University of Central Lancashire at every stage of the publishing process.

BA Publishing and MA Publishing students are based within our company and work on producing books as part of their course – some of which are selected to be published and printed by UCLan Publishing. Students also gain first-hand experience of negotiating with buyers, conceiving and running innovative high-level events to leverage sales, as well as running content creation business enterprises.

Our approach to business and teaching has been recognised academically and within the publishing industry. We have been awarded Best Newcomer at the Independent Publishing Guild Awards (2019) and a Times Higher Education Award for Excellence and Innovation in the Arts (2018).

As our business continues to grow, so too does the experience our students have upon entering UCLan Publishing. To find out more, please visit
www.uclanpublishing.com/courses